DATE DUE

OCT 0 3 2017

Return Material Promptly

SKI JUMPING

THE STORY OF CANADIANS IN THE OLYMPIC WINTER GAMES

Written by Blaine Wiseman

Weigl

Published by Weigl Educational Publishers Limited
6325 10 Street SE
Calgary, Alberta
T2H 2Z9

www.weigl.com

Library and Archives Canada Cataloguing in Publication data available upon request.
Fax 403-233-7769 for the attention of the Publishing Records department.

ISBN 978-1-55388-947-2 (hard cover)
ISBN 978-1-55388-956-4 (soft cover)

Printed in the United States of America
1 2 3 4 5 6 7 8 9 0   13 12 11 10 09

Editor: Heather C. Hudak
Design: Terry Paulhus

All of the Internet URLs given in the book were valid at the time of publication. However, due to the dynamic nature of the Internet, some
addresses may have changed, or sites may have ceased to exist since publication. While the author and publisher regret any inconvenience
this may cause readers, no responsibility for any such changes can be accepted by either the author or the publisher.

Every reasonable effort has been made to trace ownership and to obtain permission to reprint copyright material. The publishers would be
pleased to have any errors or omissions brought to their attention so that they may be corrected in subsequent printings.

Weigl acknowledges Getty Images as its primary image supplier for this title.

We gratefully acknowledge the financial support of the Government of Canada through the Book Publishing Industry Development Progra
(BPIDP) for our publishing activities.

Contents

What are the Olympic Winter Games?

The Olympic Games began more than 2,000 years ago in the town of Olympia in Ancient Greece. The Olympics were held every four years in August or September and were a showcase of **amateur** athletic talent. The games continued until 393 AD, when they were stopped by the Roman emperor.

The Olympics were not held again for more than 1,500 years. In 1896, the first modern Olympics took place in Athens, Greece. The Games were the idea of Baron Pierre de Coubertin of France. The first modern Games did not include any winter events.

In 1924, the first Olympic Winter Games were held at Chamonix, France. The Games featured 16 nations, including Canada, the United States, Finland, France, and Norway. There were 258 athletes competing in 16 events, such as skiing, ice hockey, and speed skating. That year, Jacob Tullin Thams of Norway won the first gold medal in Olympic ski jumping.

Showcasing the talents of ski jumpers from nations around the world, ski jumping is one of the most recognizable Winter Olympic sports. In this sport, athletes ski down a snow-covered hill at very high speeds before launching off a ramp and flying through the air. The best ski jumpers in the world can jump more than 200 metres. Although Canada has been represented in ski jumping at every Olympics from 1928 until 1992 and again in 2006, a Canadian has never won an Olympic medal.

Ski jumping is the only Olympic sport that does not include women in the competition. In 2009, women's ski jumping became a part of the World Ski Championships, and these athletes hope to compete in the 2014 Olympic Winter Games.

❋ CANADIAN TIDBIT
Vancouver will be the third Canadian city to host the Olympic Games. Montreal hosted the Summer Games in 1976, and Calgary hosted the Winter Games in 1988.

TOP 10 MEDAL-WINNING COUNTRIES

COUNTRY	MEDALS
Norway	280
United States	216
USSR	194
Austria	185
Germany	158
Finland	151
Canada	119
Sweden	118
Switzerland	118
Democratic Republic of Germany	110

CANADA
119

UNITED STATES
216

Winter Olympic Sports

Currently, there are seven Olympic winter sports, with a total of 15 **disciplines**. All 15 disciplines are listed here. In addition, there are five Paralympic sports. These are alpine skiing, cross-country skiing, **biathlon**, ice sledge hockey, and wheelchair curling.

Alpine Skiing

Biathlon

Bobsleigh

Cross-Country Skiing

Curling

Figure Skating

Freestyle Skiing

Ice Hockey

Luge

Nordic Combined

Short Track Speed Skating

Skeleton

Ski Jumping

Snowboarding

Speed Skating

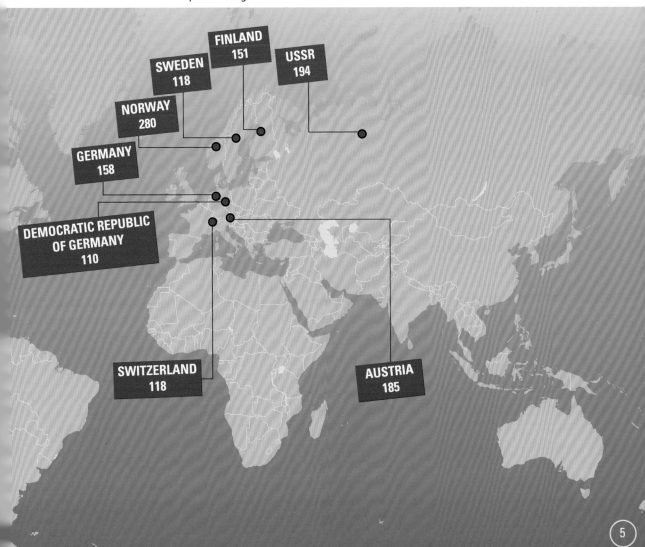

FINLAND
151

SWEDEN
118

USSR
194

NORWAY
280

GERMANY
158

DEMOCRATIC REPUBLIC
OF GERMANY
110

SWITZERLAND
118

AUSTRIA
185

Canadian Olympic Ski Jumping

Ski jumping was first done as a sport in Norway in the 19th century. When Norwegians began **immigrating** to Western Canada, they brought their skis and their passion for this sport along with them.

The first ski jumping club in Canada was formed in 1891, in Revelstoke, British Columbia. Due to its location in the Rocky Mountains, Revelstoke was popular with Norwegian immigrants, as it has perfect winter conditions for all types of skiing. The first Canadian ski jumping championship was held in Rossland, British Columbia, in 1898. Olaus Jeldness was crowned champion.

The spectacular nature of ski jumping made it very popular across Canada, and thousands of people would watch competitions. Even on the Prairies, where there are no hills large enough for ski jumping, people would build huge wooden ramps to launch themselves into the air on their skis.

During World War I, two ski clubs in Ottawa competed against each other in ski jumping. Competitors would land their jumps on the frozen Ottawa River. At one competition in Hull, Quebec, ski jumpers performed aerial stunts in front of more than 10,000

Matti Nykanen was the first ski jumper to win two gold medals in the same Olympics.

The 2010 Olympics will be Stefan Read's second chance to bring home gold.

In 1988, Canada hosted the Winter Olympics for the first time. The Games were held in Calgary, Alberta.

Matti Nykanen celebrated his team's victory in the 90-metre competition at the 1988 Olympics.

spectators. The rivalry between the ski clubs made the sport even more popular.

Even though Canada has not yet won an Olympic ski jumping medal, it has produced a number of talented jumpers. In 1925, Nels Nelson of Revelstoke set the world amateur ski jump record with a jump of 68.3 metres. Eight years later, Nelson's student, Bob Lymbourne, set a new world record when he jumped 87.5 metres. Despite early interest in the sport, ski jumping's popularity in Canada fell over the next 50 years, until Horst Bulau won the world junior championship in 1979. The next year, another Canadian, Steve Collins, won the championship.

When Calgary hosted the Winter Olympics in 1988, a new ski jumping facility was built at Canada Olympic Park, and more than 80,000 people watched the ski jumping events in Calgary. Bulau finished in seventh place, higher than any Canadian before or since.

In 2006, Canada competed in Winter Olympic ski jumping for its first time since 1992. Stefan Read was Canada's top competitor, finishing 30th. The Canadian team finished in 15th place.

✦ **CANADIAN TIDBIT** In 1913, the Great Ski Hill was built in Revelstoke. It was the largest ski jumping venue in North America.

All The Right Equipment

Skis are the most important piece of equipment in ski jumping, but because the sport is very dangerous, safety equipment is needed to protect athletes from serious injuries.

Jumping skis are heavier and longer than alpine or cross-country skis. The extra weight and length help jumpers remain stable while they soar through the air. The skis also stand up better to the impact of landing.

Skiers use bindings to attach their boots to jumping skis. Only the toe of the boot attaches to the binding so that ski jumpers can lift their heels and lean forward as they fly through the air. This technique helps skiers become more **aerodynamic**. The bindings have a connection cord that attaches to the skis and keeps them from quivering during the flight. If the skis quiver, they will cause wind resistance and make the jump shorter.

Another piece of equipment that helps ski jumpers with aerodynamics is the suit that they wear. Wearing a tight-fitting suit means that less wind catches the clothing, helping the jumper cut through the air. Ski jumping suits are made of lightweight materials that cover the entire body, except the head.

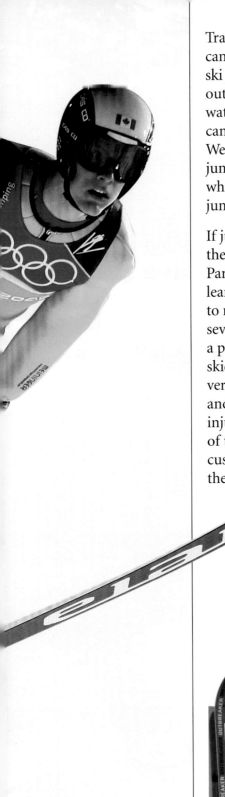

Travelling at high speeds can be hard on the eyes of ski jumpers. Wind can dry out the eyes, causing them to water. Snow or other debris can be hazards as well. Wearing goggles ensures jumpers' eyes are not harmed while they perform their jumps and landings.

If jumpers fall while landing, they can be seriously injured. Part of being a ski jumper is learning how to fall properly to reduce the chance and severity of injuries. Wearing a proper helmet protects the skier's head. Head injuries are very common in ski jumping, and helmets reduce head injuries by taking the force of the blow and cushioning the head.

Ski jumping skis are made of wood and fibreglass.

✦ **CANADIAN TIDBIT** The best ski-jumping equipment can be very expensive. Canadian ski jumpers who compete in international events rely on **sponsors** to help them pay for the equipment necessary to compete at a high level.

Qualifying to Compete

Michael "Eddie the Eagle" Edwards was the first-ever Olympic ski jumper from Great Britain.

Ski jumpers must perform at a high level for the entire year leading up to the Olympics if they want to be chosen for their national team. In the Olympics, there are three ski jumping events. These are normal hill, large hill, and team large hill.

In total, there are 75 places available for competitors in Olympic ski jumping. These are divided among the competing nations, which then select the jumpers that will represent them at the Olympics. Each participating country can send one team of six jumpers, with no more than four competitors in each competition. This means that of all the ski jumpers in Canada, only a maximum of six will be chosen to compete in the Winter Olympics.

Simply being chosen by their country is not enough for a ski jumper to qualify for the Olympics. In the season leading up to the Olympics, there are a number of International Ski Federation (FIS) World Cup and Grand Prix events that count toward Olympic qualifications. Ski jumpers must achieve points in these competitions in order to qualify for the Olympics. If a team has more ski jumpers who qualify than are allowed to compete, that team must choose which jumpers will represent the country at the Olympics.

A skier can lose up to five points for undue movement or poor form while in mid-flight.

ifty skiers take part in the first round of competition. After the first round, the 30 best skiers advance to the second round. The final core is based on both jumps.

UDGING

ki jumpers are idged on both the istance they cover the air and on the control and tyle of the jump. hey receive the ost points for ell executed, long imps. There are ve judges at competition. /hile the ski imper is in the air, judges ward points for ski control and ody control. This means that kiers who remain still and level the air will receive more oints. If the skis move around the skiers look out of control,

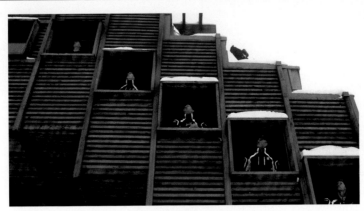

Judges watch jumpers from a special tower.

they will lose points. Jumpers also are judged on the technique, control, and ease of the landing. If jumpers land in control and with the proper technique, they will be awarded high points. If they stumble on the landing, jumpers will lose

points. Each judge gives jumpers points for control and style, which they add together. The final score for each jumper is calculated by adding together all of the judges' scores. The top and bottom scores are removed from this calculation, leaving three judges' scores to be added together. Along with points for style and control of the jump, ski jumpers are awarded points for distance. Distance points are awarded according to a mathematic formula.

Rules of Ski Jumping

The rules of ski jumping are simple. The jumper with the highest combined score from two jumps is the winner of the event.

At each ski jumping competition, there is a line drawn in the snow in the landing area. This line is called the critical point, or the K point. Distance points are based on this line. It is the ski jumper's goal to land past the K point. Jumpers are awarded 60 points for landing on the K point, and they receive additional points based on the distance they land past this point. In the normal hill competition, the K point is measured at 90 metres from the edge of the ski jump ramp. The large hill K point is measured at 120 metres.

For every 3 metres that jumpers land past the K point in the large hill event, they are awarded 1.8 points. For example, if a jumper clears the K point by 6 metres, he will be awarded 3.6 additional points.

In the normal hill event, jumpers are awarded 2 points per 3 metres rather than 1.8 points.

In 2006, Norwegian ski jumper Sigurd Pettersen took part in the Winter Olympics.

✦ **CANADIAN TIDBIT** At the Calgary Winter Olympics in 1988, Michael Edwards of England became an international celebrity when he competed in ski jumping. Known as "Eddie the Eagle," Edwards finished in second-last place. After the Olympics, the International Olympic Committee (IOC) changed the qualifying rules so that only world-class ski jumpers could qualify. This meant that competitors, such as Edwards, who did not have sufficient training could no longer participate in Olympic ski jumping competitions.

Jumpers who do not reach the K point have points deducted from their score. In large hill, for every 3 metres that jumpers land behind the K point, they have 1.8 points deducted. In normal hill, 2 points are lost.

In addition to distance measures, there are only a few other rules in ski jumping. Skiers must use the proper equipment when competing in the Olympics. If skiers use skis that exceed the legal length, they will be disqualified from the competition.

Ski-jumping skis are longer than other types of skis. They can be as long as 275 centimetres.

PERFORMANCE ENHANCING DRUGS

Although the Olympics are a celebration of excellence and sportsmanship, some athletes use performance enhancing drugs to give them an unfair advantage over other athletes. There are many different types of performance enhancing drugs, including steroids. Some make muscles bigger, others help muscles recover more quickly, while some can make athletes feel less pain, giving them more **endurance**. The International

Olympic Committee (IOC) takes the use of performance enhancing drugs very seriously. Regular testing of athletes helps ensure competitors do not use drugs to unnaturally improve their skills. Ski jumping requires a mixture of strength, speed, and endurance. Many performance-enhancing drugs will help an athlete in one of these areas, but hurt them in others. For example, a drug may cause the heart to pump more blood to muscles in the arms, making the athlete physically stronger. This takes

blood away from the heart and lungs, giving the athlete less endurance and slower long-term recovery. There are serious mental and physical health problems that arise from using these drugs, such as sleep problems, sickness, and high blood pressure. Athletes who use steroids for a long time may die early from heart attacks and other problems.

Exploring the Venue

Whistler consistently ranks as one of the top five ski resorts in North America and is the only resort in North America where people can ski down a glacier.

Olympic events are held in huge, specially built venues around the host city. These buildings can be used to exhibit one or multiple events and can cost more than $1 billion to build.

CEREMONIES

Two of the most-anticipated and popular events of the Olympics are the opening and closing ceremonies. These events are traditionally held in the largest venue that an Olympic host city can offer. Facilities such as football, baseball, or soccer stadiums are often used for these events. At the 2008 Olympic Games in Beijing, more than 90,000 people attended the opening ceremonies. The ceremonies are spectacular displays that include music, dancing, acrobatic stunts, and fireworks. The theme of the ceremonies usually celebrates the history and culture of the host nation and city. All of the athletes participating in the Olympics march into the stadium during the ceremonies. The athletes wave their country's flag and celebrate the achievement of competing in the Olympics.

The ski jumps at Whistler are classified as HS 125. This notation indicates the distance skiers should be able to jump consistently from ramps.

Due to the sport's popularity with spectators, ski jumping venues must be able to hold thousands of people. The large size of the jumps requires ski jumping venues to be built outdoors. Fans crowd around the jumping and landing zones in order to watch the athletes soar through the air.

The ski jumping venue for the 2010 Olympics is Whistler Olympic Park. The park features two large ski jumps that are built side-by-side. Building these ski jumps took 750 tons of steel.

There are two sizes of jumps used in the Olympics. These are the large hill and the normal hill. Skiers can achieve a maximum flight distance of 140 metres on the larger of Whistler's two ramps. On the smaller ramp, a ski jumper's maximum flight distance is 106 metres. Only the best jumpers will be able to achieve these distances.

✦ **CANADIAN TIDBIT** The Olympic Stadium in Montreal is one of the most expensive stadiums ever built. By the time it was paid off in 2006, the building had cost more than $1.4 billion.

TECHNIQUE

From starting gate to landing, a ski jump lasts between 5 and 8 seconds. During that brief period, jumpers are expected to maintain both stance and balance: arms close to the body, skis horizontal and spread in a V shape during flight, then the telemark position, and a controlled outrun until they come to a stop at the safety fence. The judges deduct style points for uneven skis, flapping arms during flight to retain balance, and premature preparation for landing.

1. INRUN
The jumper drops into an aerodynamic crouch, and maintains that position until the takeoff point. Skiers attain speeds of over 80 km/h on K90 hills, and over 90 km/h on K120 hills.

2. TAKEOFF
This is the critical point of the jump: taking off too early or too late can substantially reduce distance. The jumper has to stretch out immediately upon reaching the takeoff point. The skier's body straightens out very quickly and leans forward.

3. FLIGHT
The skier leans forward toward the tip of the skis to reduce drag. The tips are spread, creating a V shape to provide greater lift and distance for the flight. Between takeoff and landing, the skier is in the air for 2 or 3 seconds.

4. LANDING
The force of the landing is the equivalent of 3 times the skier's weight. The telemark position (one leg slightly in front of the other) allows the shock to be absorbed by the forward leg and flow through the entire body before the skier is steady enough to start braking.

THE K POINT

The K point marks the length of an ideal, theoretical jump. It represents the recommended landing point, which is used as a reference and is located where the slope begins to flatten out. The distance between the K point and the end of the ramp is 90 m on a normal hill, and 120 m on a large hill.

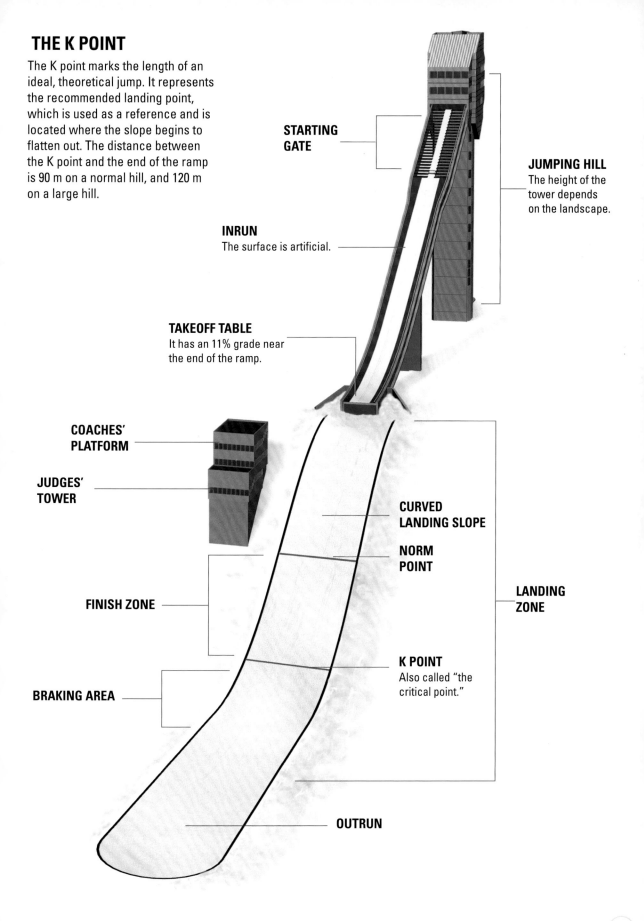

STARTING GATE

JUMPING HILL
The height of the tower depends on the landscape.

INRUN
The surface is artificial.

TAKEOFF TABLE
It has an 11% grade near the end of the ramp.

COACHES' PLATFORM

JUDGES' TOWER

FINISH ZONE

BRAKING AREA

CURVED LANDING SLOPE

NORM POINT

LANDING ZONE

K POINT
Also called "the critical point."

OUTRUN

Olympic Legends

Jacob Tullin Thams

In 1924, Jacob Tullin Thams won the first Olympic Winter Games ski jumping gold medal at the Games in Chamonix, France. Thams won the normal hill event, beating 26 other competitors. At the next Winter Olympics, Thams and his Norwegian teammates were disappointed when they saw that the ski jump had a longer run than usual. This allowed skiers to gain greater speed on the ramp. Thams felt that this gave an unfair advantage to less-skilled ski jumpers. However, on his second jump, Thams jumped 73 metres, farther than anyone had ever jumped before. He jumped so far that he missed the landing slope and fell. The fall dropped him to 28th place, but Thams had proven his jumping ability. Thams' final Olympics were the 1936 Summer Games in Berlin, Germany. He won a silver medal in **yachting**, along with his Norwegian teammates. Thams is one of only four people to win medals in both the Summer and Winter Olympics.

FAST FACT

Thams' two Olympic gold-winning jumps were each 49 metres.

OLYMPIC MEDALS WON

1 Gold   1 Silver

Matti Nykanen

Although he only appeared in two Olympic Winter Games, Matti Nykanen of Finland had an amazing ski jumping career. At the 1984 Winter Olympics in Sarajevo, Yugoslavia, Nykanen dominated the large hill event. He won by 17.5 points, the biggest difference between first and second place in Olympic ski-jumping history. Nykanen also won a silver medal in the normal hill event. At the following Olympics in Calgary, Nykanen repeated his gold-medal performance, this time winning by 17 points. He then won the normal hill event by 16.5 points. The victory made Nykanen the first ski jumper to win two gold medals at the same Olympics. That same year, a team ski jumping event was introduced to the Olympics. Nykanen and his Finnish teammates won the gold medal, giving him his third gold medal of the games. In total, Nykanen won four gold medals and one silver in his two Olympic appearances.

FAST FACT

Ski jumping experts believe that Nykanen's broad yet thin body gave him an advantage over other skiers and made him naturally built for ski jumping.

OLYMPIC MEDALS WON

4 Gold   1 Silver

OLYMPIC MEDALS WON

2 Gold   1 Bronze

Toni Nieminen

In 1992, at the Olympics in Albertville, France, Toni Nieminen became the youngest male athlete to win a gold medal in the history of the Olympic Winter Games. At only 16 years of age, Nieminen helped his Finnish teammates win the team large hill event. It was the second straight gold medal in the event for Finland. Only two days later, Nieminen made history again when he won the gold medal in the large hill event. He was the youngest male athlete to win gold in an individual event. Nieminen beat the previous record by almost two years. He also won the bronze medal in the normal hill event. Due to his success, Nieminen became an instant celebrity in Finland. In 1994, he became the first ski jumper to jump more than 200 metres. In 2002, 10 years after his first appearance in the Games, he competed in his second Winter Olympics, but did not repeat his medal-winning performance.

OLYMPIC MEDALS WON

3 Gold   1 Silver

Jens Weissflog

German ski jumper Jens Weissflog had a very successful first appearance at the Winter Olympics. In 1984, Weissflog won the gold medal in the normal hill event and silver in the large hill event. When a new ski-jumping technique was invented by Sweden's Jan Boklov, Weissflog had trouble adapting. He competed at the next two Winter Olympics but could not match the success he enjoyed in 1984. In fact, his best finish at these Games was 9th place. At his final Olympics, in 1994, Weissflog used the Boklov technique to launch a spectacular second jump in the large hill event. As a result, he overcame a 10.3-point deficit to win the gold medal. Later, Weissflog and his German teammates also won gold in the team large hill event. Weissflog won his second and third Olympic gold medals 10 years after winning his first.

Visit the FIS ski jumping website at **www.fis-ski.com/uk/disciplines/ skijumping.html**.

Learn more about Eddie the Eagle at **http://archives.cbc.ca/sports/olympics/ topics/1322-8081**.

Olympic Stars

Stefan Read

Canada's Stefan Read has skiing in his blood. Read's uncle, Ken, is a Canadian skiing legend. Known as one of the "Crazy Canucks," Ken helped put Canada on the map in alpine skiing. Stefan hopes to do the same in ski jumping. Read will be competing in his second Winter Olympics and represents Canada's best hope for a medal in ski jumping. At his first Winter Olympics, in 2006, Read finished in 30th place in the large hill competition and 42nd in normal hill. Read and his Canadian teammates finished 15th in the team large hill event.

In preparing for the 2010 Olympics, Read qualified for the World Cup Circuit.

FAST FACT

Read currently resides in Calgary, Alberta.

Gregor Schlierenzauer

Gregor Schlierenzauer has dominated the 2009 World Cup of ski jumping in preparation for the Winter Olympics in 2010. Schlierenzauer, who is only 19, has won three world championships in his young career. Schlierenzauer, known by his nickname "Schlieri," hopes to lead his Austrian ski jumping team to success at Whistler in 2010. In 2009, he was ranked as the top ski jumper in the world.

FAST FACT

Schlierenzauer became the youngest Ski Flying World Champion in Oberstdorf, Germany.

Simon Ammann

Simon Ammann of Switzerland took part in his first Winter Olympics in 1998, in Nagano, Japan. He finished in 39th place in large hill and 35th in normal hill. Leading up to the 2002 Olympics in Salt Lake City, Utah, Ammann had not won a World Cup event. In fact, Ammann's best finish in a normal hill event was 26th place. Ammann surprised the world when he won the gold medal in the normal hill event by 1.5 points. Many people thought that Ammann's victory had more to do with luck than skill. However, four days later, he silenced many of his critics by winning the gold medal in the large hill event as well. This time, Ammann won by more than 11 points. In 2006, Ammann did not win an Olympic medal. He did, however, win the 2006 ski jumping World Cup.

FAST FACT

At the 2002 Olympics, Ammann became the youngest jumper to win two gold medals in the same Olympics.

MEDALS WON

2 Gold

Andreas Kuettel

At the Winter Olympics in 2006, Switzerland's Andreas Kuettel finished just outside of the medals in both individual ski-jumping events. In the normal hill and large hill events, Kuettel finished in 6th place. He also finished in 6th place in the large hill event at the Olympics in 2002. Kuettel has been competing in the World Cup of ski jumping since 1995, and in 2009, won his first World Championship in the large hill event.

FAST FACT

Kuettel soared an astounding 133.5 metres to win gold at the 2009 World Championships.

UANT MORE?

For up-to-date information on ski jumping, check out **www.ctvolympics.ca/ski-jumping/news/index.html**.

For information about Canadian ski jumping, check out **www.skijumpingcanada.com**.

A Day in the Life of an Olympic Athlete

Becoming an Olympic athlete takes a great deal of dedication and **perseverance**. Athletes must concentrate on remaining healthy and maximizing their strength and energy. Eating special foods according to a strict schedule, taking vitamins, waking up early to train and practise, and going to bed at a reasonable hour are important parts of staying in shape for world-class athletes. All athletes have different routines and training regimens. These regimens are suited to that athlete's body and lifestyle.

Eggs are a great source of **protein** and **iron**, and are low in **calories**, making them a popular breakfast choice. A cup of orange juice is a healthy breakfast drink, while coffee can give an athlete some extra energy in the morning. A light lunch, including a sandwich, yogurt, fruit, and juice, is usually a good option. This gives the body the right amount of energy, while it is not too filling. Chicken and pasta are popular dinnertime meals.

Athletes who regularly eat a nutritious breakfast have higher energy levels than those who do not.

Early Mornings

6:30 a.m.

Olympic athletes might wake up at 6:30 a.m. to record their resting **heart rate**. Next, they might stretch or perform yoga while their breakfast is preparing. The first exercise of the day can happen before 7:00 a.m. Depending on an athlete's sport, the exercise routine can vary. A skier might be in the gym lifting weights. After lifting weights for an hour, the athlete may move on to **aerobics** to help with strength and endurance.

Morning Practice

9:30 a.m.

By about 9:30 a.m., athletes are ready to practise their event. For a ski jumper, this means putting on skis and hitting the jumps. Most Olympic athletes have coaches and trainers who help them develop training routines. After practice, ski jumpers stretch to keep their muscles loose and avoid injuries. Many athletes use a sauna or an ice bath to help their muscles recover quickly.

Afternoon Nap

12:00 p.m.

At about noon, many athletes choose to take a break. Sleep helps the body and mind recover from stress. After waking up at 2:00 p.m., it is time for lunch and then, more exercise. **Core** exercises using special equipment help ski jumpers with stability. Working out the leg muscles is an important part of training for skiers.

Dinnertime

6:00 p.m.

After the afternoon workout, it is dinnertime. Another healthy meal helps athletes recover from the day and prepare their body for the next day's training. The evening can be spent relaxing and doing more light stretches. It is important for athletes to rest after a hard day of training so that they can do their challenging routine again the next day.

Olympic Volunteers

Biglietteria
Ticket Box Office

Volunteers sweep and shovel snow in order to make the Olympics safe and enjoyable for everyone.

Olympic volunteers are dedicated individuals who are specially selected by the committee. They go above and beyond to ensure the Olympics run smoothly as possible.

Volunteers are an important part of creating an enjoyable Olympic experience for athletes and spectators. Thousands of volunteers help organize and execute the Olympic Games. Olympic volunteers are enthusiastic, committed, and dedicated to helping welcome the world to the host city. Volunteers help prepare for the Olympics in the years leading up to the events.

Before the Olympics begin, many countries send representatives to the host city to view event venues and plans. Olympic volunteers help make the representatives' stay enjoyable. From meeting these representatives at the airport, showing them around the city and the surrounding areas, and providing accommodations and transportation, volunteers make life easier for visitors to the host city.

✦ **CANADIAN TIDBIT** About 25,000 volunteers are helping with the Olympics in Vancouver. They will make sure the games are a memorable, enjoyable experience for athletes, judges, spectators, and officials from all over the world.

During the Olympics, volunteers help in many different areas. During the opening, closing, and medal ceremonies, volunteers help prepare costumes, props, and performers for the events. Editorial volunteers help by preparing written materials for use in promoting events and on the official website of the Olympics. Food and beverage volunteers provide catering services to athletes, judges, officials, spectators, and media.

Some volunteers get a chance to view events and work with competitors. Anti-doping volunteers notify athletes when they have been selected for drug testing. These volunteers explain the process to the athletes and escort them to the drug-testing facility. Other volunteers get to be involved with the sporting events by helping to maintain the venues and the fields of play, providing medical assistance to athletes, transporting athletes to events, and helping with the set-up and effective running of events.

Once lit, the Olympic torch is left lit until the Games conclude.

TORCH RELAY

One of the most anticipated events of each Olympics is the torch relay. The torch is lit during a ritual in Olympia, Greece, before it is flown to the host nation. The torch is then carried along a route across the country, until it reaches the host city during the opening ceremonies. The torch relay for 2010 covers 45,000 kilometres over 106 days. The relay will begin in Victoria before moving through communities in all 10 Canadian provinces and three territories. About 12,000 volunteers will be chosen to carry the torch across Canada. Other volunteers help drive and maintain the vehicles that accompany the torch on its journey.

What are the Paralympics?

First held in 1960, the Paralympic Games are a sports competition for disabled competitors. Like the Olympics, the Paralympics celebrate the athletic achievements of its competitors. The Paralympics are held in the same year and city as the Olympics. Many sports appear in both the Paralympics and the Olympics, such as swimming, nordic skiing, and alpine skiing. The Paralympics also feature wheelchair basketball, **goalball**, and ice sledge hockey. The first Winter Paralympic Games were held in 1976.

Athletes competing at the Paralympics are classified by disability in six categories, including **amputee**, **cerebral palsy**, **visual impairment**, **spinal cord** injuries, **intellectual disability**, and a group for other disabilities. These classifications allow athletes to compete in a fair and equal basis in each event. Goalball, for example, is a sport for the visually impaired, not for amputees.

Sit-skis originated in Scandinavia more than 4,000 years ago as a form of transportation through snow. Eventually, they were modified to give wheelchair-bound athletes the ability to ski.

Ice sledge hockey is traditionally a men's sport. However, women will be allowed to compete for the first time in ice sledge hockey at the 2010 Olympics.

Wheelchair curling has been an Olympic sport since the Turin games in 2006.

Some Paralympic sports use specially adapted equipment. Ice sledge hockey is a sport for people with disabled legs. Players sit on a special sled, or sledge, with two blades on the bottom side that allow the puck to pass underneath. Players use two small hockey sticks to push themselves along the ice and to handle the puck. One end of the stick has a blade like a regular hockey stick, and the other end has a spike. The blade end is used to handle the puck, and the players dig the spike into the ice to propel themselves around the rink. Alpine skiers have specially built ski poles with small skis on the bottom. This sport is for people who have had a leg amputated. Skiers use the poles to help push them along, as well as to balance them.

To turn the sit-ski, skiers drag one pole in the snow and lean in the direction they want to turn.

Olympics and the Environment

Hosting so many people in one city can be costly to the environment. Host cities often build new venues and roads to accommodate the Games. For example, a great deal of transportation is needed to support construction projects, planning for the games, and to move the athletes, participants, volunteers, media, and spectators around the host city and its surrounding areas. This transportation causes pollution.

In recent years, the IOC and Olympic host cities have been working to make the Olympics more green. With their beautiful surroundings, including the Pacific Ocean to the West and the Rocky Mountains to the East, Vancouver and Whistler have taken many steps to protect the environment.

Vancouver is known around the world for its sustainability programs.

WHISTLER SLIDING CENTRE

At the Whistler Sliding Centre, home to the bobsleigh, luge, and skeleton events, an ice plant is used to keep the ice frozen. The heat waste from this plant is used to heat other buildings in the area. All wood waste from the Whistler sites will be chipped, composted, and reused on the same site.

LIL'WAT ABORIGINAL NATION

Working with the Lil'wat Aboriginal Nation, builders of the Olympic cross-country ski trails created venues that could be used long after the Olympics. About 50 kilometres of trails have been built that can be used by cross-country skiers and hikers of all skill levels.

VANCOUVER LIGHTING AND HEATING SYSTEMS

Venues in Whistler and Vancouver have been equipped with efficient lighting and heating systems. These systems reduce the amount of **greenhouse gases** released into the atmosphere during the Olympics.

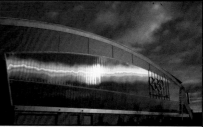

GREENHOUSE GASES

Half of the organizing committee's vehicles are either **hybrid** or equipped with fuel management technology. These vehicles emit less greenhouse gases than other vehicles. As well, venues have been made accessible to users of transit, and many event tickets include transit tickets to promote mass transportation at the games.

VANCOUVER CONVENTION AND EXHIBITION CENTRE

The Vancouver Convention and Exhibition Centre uses a seawater heating system. This system uses the surrounding natural resources to make the building a more comfortable place to visit. The centre also houses a fish habitat.

RICHMOND OLYMPIC OVAL

The Richmond Olympic Oval was built with a wooden arced ceiling. The huge amount of wood needed to build the ceiling was reclaimed from forests that have been destroyed by mountain pine beetles. These beetles feed on pine trees, killing them in the process. Using this wood helps stop other, healthy trees from being cut down for construction materials.

✸ **CANADIAN TIDBIT** The 2010 Games are estimated to cost more than $4 billion, including about $2.5 billion of taxpayer money.

Build Your Own Ski Jump

Ski jump builders use math and science to ensure the venues they build will help ski jumpers fly through the air. You can build a miniature ramp to see how changing a few angles makes a difference in the distance and height ski jumpers can achieve.

What you need

baking sheet or large piece cardboard
thick, hard cover book
sheet of paper
marble or a small ball

1. Lean the baking sheet or piece of cardboard against a couch, chair, or desk. This will act as a ramp.

2. Place the book at the bottom of the ramp. This is the jump. Make sure that the top of the jump is higher than the bottom of the ramp. This will help launch the "ski jumper" into the air.

3. Use a piece of paper to smooth the edge between the ramp and the jump.

4. Place the marble or ball at the top of the ramp, and let go. This will be your "ski jumper."

5. Mark where the "ski jumper" lands by placing a piece of paper labelled "#1" on the floor.

6. Now, try leaning the ramp at a steeper angle, and drop the marble or ball from the top. Where does it land this time? Mark the spot with a piece of paper labelled "#2."

7. Raise the jump, and repeat step 4. Mark where the "ski jumper" lands with a piece of paper labelled "#3."

8. Try using different materials to make the ramp longer and the jump shorter. By changing the length and angle of the ramp and the jump, you are experimenting with **physics**.

Further Research

Visit Your Library

Many books and websites provide information on ski jumping. To learn more about ski jumping, borrow books from the library, or surf the Internet.

Most libraries have computers that connect to a database for researching information. If you input a key word, you will be provided with a list of books in the library that contain information on that topic. Nonfiction books are arranged numerically, using their call number. Fiction books are organized alphabetically by the author's last name.

Surf the Web

Learn more about ski jumping by visiting **www.olympic.org/uk/sports/programme/ history_uk.asp?DiscCode=SJ&sportCode =SI**.

To learn all about the 2010 Winter Olympics, visit **www.vancouver2010.com**.

Glossary

aerobics: exercise for the heart and lungs

aerodynamic: reducing the amount of drag from air resistance

amateur: an athlete who does not receive money for competing

amputee: a person who has had a body part removed

biathlon: a sport in which athletes combine cross-country skiing and target shooting skills

calories: units of energy, especially in food

cerebral palsy: a condition that typically causes impaired muscle coordination

core: the trunk of the body, including the hips and torso

disciplines: subdivisions within a sport that require different skills, training, or equipment

endurance: the ability to continue doing something that is difficult

goalball: a sport for blind athletes; the ball used makes noise, helping blind athletes locate it

greenhouse gases: gases that trap the Sun's energy in Earth's atmosphere, causing the greenhouse effect

heart rate: the number of times the heart beats in one minute

hybrid: a vehicle that uses a combination of fuels

immigrating: moving to another country

intellectual disability: a disability that hampers the function of the mind

iron: a substance in foods that is good for the blood

perseverance: a commitment to doing a task despite challenges that arise in the process

physics: the science of matter and energy and how they interact

protein: a substance needed by the body to build healthy muscles

spinal cord: a bundle of nerves held inside the spine, connecting almost all parts of the body to the brain

sponsors: companies that help athletes by giving them merchandise or living expenses

visual impairment: not being able to see well

yachting: a sport in which competitors race sailboats

Index